MR. MEN
LITTLE MISS
Hospital

Roger Hargreaves

Original concept by
Roger Hargreaves

Written and illustrated by
Adam Hargreaves

EGMONT

Mr Bump had learnt a lot of things in his life.

To never set foot on a skateboard.

To never climb ladders.

And to never bounce on a trampoline.

But yesterday morning, he made a mistake and banged his head and had to go to hospital in an ambulance.

The ambulance driver was Little Miss Quick, so they got to the hospital before you could say 'quick sticks'!

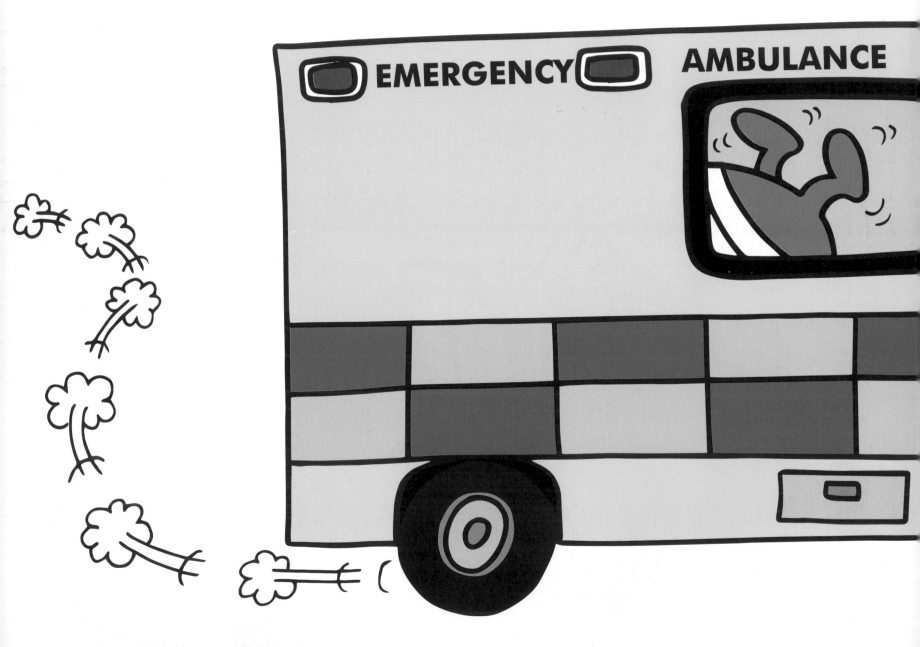

Which was nearly as fast as the porter who rushed him into Accident and Emergency on a stretcher.

The porter was Mr Rush.

"Hello, Mr Bump," said Doctor Happy.

Everyone at the hospital knew Mr Bump.

Being the accidental fellow he was, he was there nearly every day.

Doctor Happy checked him over and then Nurse Naughty
bandaged him up.

Bandages on bandages!

The next person to arrive at hospital was Mr Silly.

Doctor Happy could not believe his eyes, he had never seen a case like Mr Silly's.

"How on earth did that happen?" he asked.

But it was probably best not to ask!

There were many reasons why people ended up at the hospital.

Mr Tall had hurt his leg and needed an X-ray to look at the bones.

However, with Mr Impossible as the doctor, he didn't have to go to the X-ray room.

Doctor Impossible has X-Ray vision!

Mr Tall had broken his leg and it needed to be set in plaster.

An awful lot of plaster!

Poor Mr Tall had to walk with crutches.

Extraordinarily long crutches!

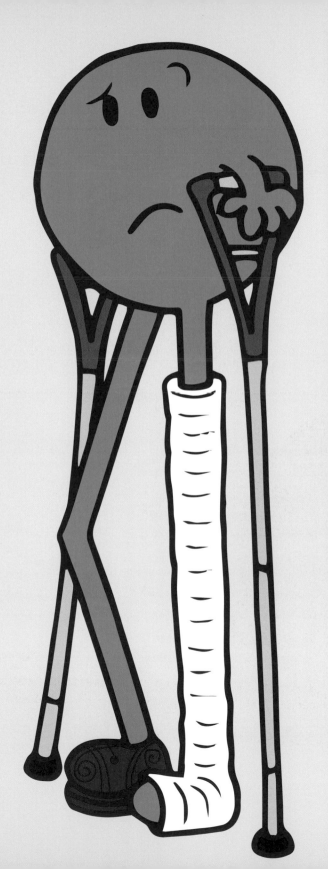

There were lots of different machines in the hospital.

Mr Nobody had to have a scan, but the Doctor could not believe his eyes when he looked at the screen.

There was nothing inside Mr Nobody!

Not a thing.

"That's impossible!" cried Doctor Impossible.

Some people have impossibly difficult illnesses to diagnose.

Like Little Miss Giggles who was admitted with a rather peculiar problem.

She kept making very odd noises.

"ATISH-HIC-GIGGLE-UP-TOO! ATISH-HIC-GIGGLE-UP-TOO!"

All the doctors came to see her and they all went away scratching their heads.

What ever was wrong with Little Miss Giggles?

It took all Doctor Brainy's brainpower to work out that Little Miss Giggles had a case of the hiccups with a fit of the giggles on top of the flu!

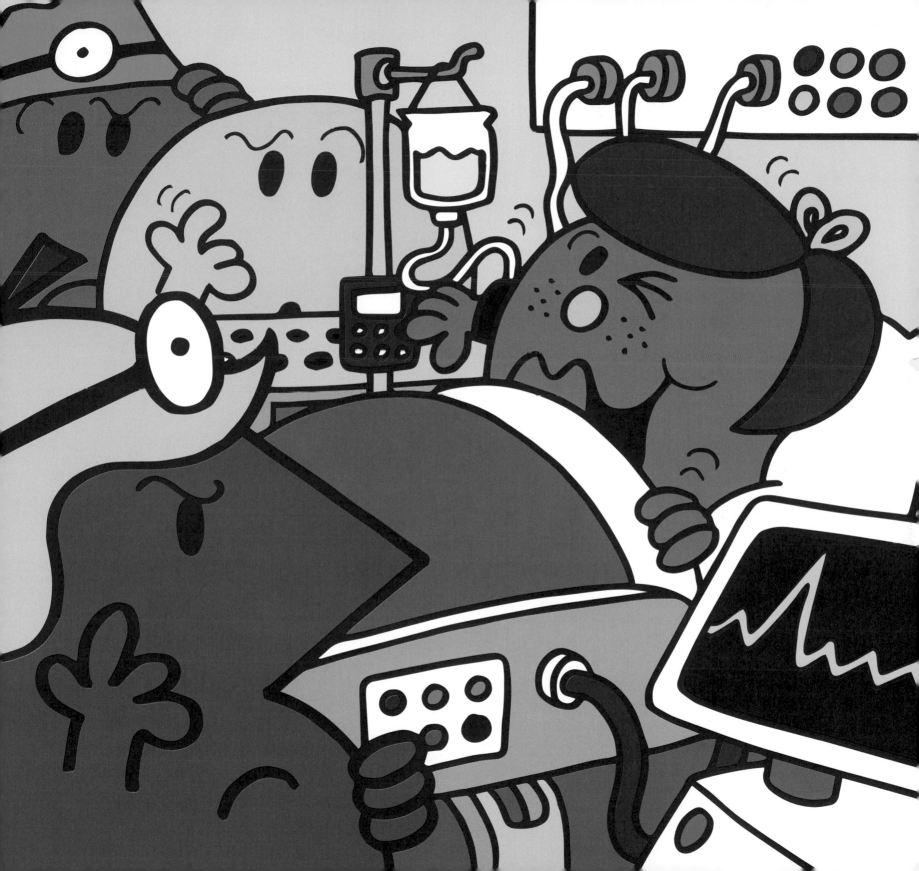

Some people were at the hospital to have an operation.

Before an operation, the operating room had to be germ free.

And the perfect person for that job was Little Miss Neat.

It was the cleanest, shiniest, neatest operating room in the world.

I don't think Mr Messy could get a job in a hospital!

The patient was given an anaesthetic to put them to sleep before their operation.

Unless the patient was Mr Lazy.

He was already fast asleep!

The operation was then performed by a surgeon, who must have a very steady hand.

I don't think Mr Jelly would make a good surgeon.

And definitely not Mr Tickle!

While the patients were getting better, they stayed in a hospital ward where the nurses looked after them.

Everything Nurse Perfect did was, of course, perfect.

And you would think that Little Miss Helpful would also make a wonderful nurse, but as helpful as Nurse Helpful tried to be, things never quite went to plan.

The head nurse on the ward was Little Miss Bossy.

Matron Bossy!

She didn't just manage the ward, she also made sure the patients behaved themselves.

Especially patients like Little Miss Trouble!

Nurse Hug worked in the maternity ward where babies were born.

She was very good at soothing all the babies.

While the patients were recuperating, they were allowed to have visitors.

Which was something to look forward to.

Unless the visitor was Little Miss Chatterbox.

Chat, chat, chat, chat, chat!

Little Miss Sunshine was very glad that the hospital had visiting hours, otherwise she might have been up all night!

Mr Greedy brought in some grapes for Mr Quiet when he went to visit him.

Which was very thoughtful, except for the fact that Mr Quiet didn't get to eat any!

I wonder why?

When it was time to leave hospital, some of the patients were wheeled to the exit in a wheelchair.

Like Mr Quiet and Little Miss Sunshine when they were all better.

However, they were wheeled out by Nurse Naughty and Mr Mischief the porter.

Who had a wheelchair race down the corridor!

Matron Bossy was not happy.

As Little Miss Sunshine and Mr Quiet were leaving, Little Miss Quick arrived in her ambulance with the sirens blaring.

And who do you think she was bringing to the hospital?

Somebody who had had an accident.

And who could that be?

Accident & Emergency

That's right!

Mr Bump!

"Back again," said Doctor Happy.